BRIGITTE AND FERDINAND

a love story by Bernadette Watts

Prentice-Hall, Inc. Englewood Cliffs, New Jersey

Prentice-Hall International, Inc., London
Prentice-Hall of Australia, Pty. Ltd., North Sydney
Prentice-Hall of Canada, Ltd., Toronto
Prentice-Hall of India Private Ltd., New Delhi
Prentice-Hall of Japan, Inc., Tokyo

0-13-081919-0

Once upon a time, there was a fluteplayer named Ferdinand.
Sometimes he played with an orchestra or a circus, and sometimes when he had no work he played his flute at a cafe to earn a few pennies.

Brigitte smiled when she saw Ferdinand and folded up the dress she was making.
"Who is that for?" Ferdinand asked.
"For Clarissa, the lovliest lady at the court," Brigitte said.
"If people think Clarissa is lovliest, they have never seen you," Ferdinand laughed.

One day the owner of a cafe gave Ferdinand a roast chicken and some wine. Ferdinand hurried to the attic where his sweetheart Brigitte the seamstress lived, to share them with her.

The kettle sang on the stove in the cozy attic. Brigitte gathered up the scraps of cloth left over from her day's work. She was saving them to make a patch-work jacket for Ferdinand.

After supper, they sat by the window gazing at the moon and stars. "When I am famous," Ferdinand said,"I will buy you a fur muff to warm you in the winter and a parasol to shade you in the summer." "And when you are famous," Brigitte said, "you will soon forget me."

The next day, as Ferdinand played in the cafe for his supper, he saw only Brigitte. When he played his flute, every note overflowed with the love he felt for the little seamstress. Everyone listened.

One person who listened very carefully was Freddie
Fisher, the conductor of an orchestra. His fat face
was scarlet with anger because his meal was taking
so long to come. But Ferdinand's music soothed him,
and then delighted him.

"Young man," he called to Ferdinand. "I like your tunes. Write them down for my orchestra, and I will pay you well."

Ferdinand stayed up all that night writing down every tune he knew. The next morning, he tied his music in a bundle, polished his boots and hurried to the Opera House to meet Freddie Fisher.

Mr. Fisher thanked Ferdinand for the pile of tunes he had written for Mr. Fisher's orchestra. He paid him with a wicked smile, thinking what a bargain he had made. Ferdinand smiled too, thinking of the wonderful presents he could buy for Brigitte.

But first, he thought, I will have a good meal. The meal was so good, it cost every penny Ferdinand had earned. Poor Ferdinand!

As he walked home penniless, Ferdinand knew what he had to do. He would write more tunes for Mr. Fisher, and with that money, he would buy something for Brigitte.

But the more money he made, the more money Ferdinand spent. There was never anything left for Brigitte. He went to more fashionable restaurants, and spent money on fancy clothes.

Ferdinand was becoming famous for his tunes. Believing that he owed everything to the wicked Freddie Fisher, the flute-player became his slave. There was no time to visit Brigitte any more.

Brigitte read the announcements for Ferdinand's concerts, but she didn't have enough money for tickets. Brigitte made fine clothes for other ladies to wear to Ferdinand's concerts, but she never went herself.

Every evening she laid out plates for supper, but Ferdinand never came. She thought of the fur muff Ferdinand had promised her for cold winter, and shivered. But she still collected scraps of cloth for Ferdinand's patchwork jacket.

One day, Ferdinand and Freddie Fisher were asked to perform at court. From the stage, Ferdinand saw the beautiful Clarissa and fell in love. He sent her jewels and flowers, and poems asking her to be his wife. And the beautiful Clarissa agreed, because Ferdinand was famous, not because she loved him.

Clarissa began planning their wedding at once. "I will have the most beautiful wedding dress in the world," she said. "It will be embroidered with pearls and over it I will wear a cloak of white fur."
"Who can make such a beautiful dress?" her maid asked.
"The shabby little girl who makes all my clothes," said Clarissa.

Brigitte began working on Clarissa's wedding dress slowly because it was so cold in her attic. "Clarissa will make a fine wife for Ferdinand," she thought as she worked," but I wish *I* were going to be his bride."

She worked very hard to make Clarissa's wedding dress the most beautiful dress in the world. While she waited for the maid to pick up the dress, she shared some bread with the sparrows shivering on the window ledge and watched the first snowflake fall.

"Please take a present to the bridegroom for me," said Brigitte to the maid. "He was once a friend of mine."

The present was the patchwork jacket which she had just finished.
"Oh, the bridegroom already has his wedding suit," said the maid. "Anyway, I cannot carry any more."

Poor Brigitte sat down on the sofa. There she fell
asleep and dreamed she was walking in a sunny
meadow.
In every tree, birds sang. Then, across the meadow
came Ferdinand.

It was the day of the wedding.
Ferdinand sat staring at the floor.
"I should be happy," he said to Freddie Fisher, "but
I feel so sorrowful that I cannot even play my flute.
Why am I so sad?"
All Freddie Fisher said was: "Here is our carriage!
See the crowds waiting to cheer us!"

The sun bathed the snowy streets in a
rosy glow and turned the roofs to gold.
In the heart of the city there were so
many people that the carriage could not
get through. So they took to the narrow
streets where the poor people lived.

"I feel so peaceful here," said Ferdinand. "Look at the children playing."

"Nonsense," said Freddie Fisher. "How it stinks! Shut the window."

Ferdinand gazed out the window longingly. In the market place, he saw a beautiful patchwork jacket. "Stop the carriage," he called. "I must have that beautiful jacket."

"Certainly," said the market woman. "It was made by a neighbor of mine who has been brokenhearted since her sweetheart left her. But a fine gentleman like you wouldn't know Ferdinand the fluteplayer."

"But I am not a fine gentleman, I am a fool. *I* am Ferdinand the fluteplayer!" he shouted.

"Hurry up!" Freddie Fisher shouted from the carriage. Ferdinand cried, "I must go and beg Brigitte's forgiveness. Oh, how could I have forgotten her? She is the sweetest person in the world and *she* will be my bride."

The little fluteplayer ran to the house where Brigitte lived. On the street corner a boy was selling flowers. "I will buy all your flowers," cried Ferdinand. But when he felt in his pocket for money, it was, as usual, empty. "Never mind," he said. "I will play my flute until I have enough money for every single one." So he took out his flute and began to play.

Meanwhile Freddie Fisher had arrived at the church. Too proud to leave without a husband, Clarissa quickly agreed to marry him.

So Freddie and Clarissa became husband and wife. And a very good match it was, too, as one was as unpleasant as the other, and the rest of their lives was spent in quarrels.

When Brigitte awoke from her deep sleep, she felt peaceful and fresh. She put on her prettiest dress. Then she heard music floating up from the square. She leaned out of the window and thought to herself, "Who is that musician wearing the patchwork jacket? I cannot see clearly. I will go down and listen."

Ferdinand played songs about swallows in summer skies, about the wind on the sea, and about Brigitte whom he saw so clearly that he believed she really stood at his side. Before long he realized that Brigitte really was standing beside him. She had never looked so beautiful.

When the moon rose, the little fluteplayer had earned all the flowers, and Brigitte laughed with joy when he gave her a cartload of lilies and snowdrops, daffodils and violets. Ferdinand gave them with all his love, for he had grown older and wiser. Then, together, they went home to the little attic where Brigitte had waited so long for the little fluteplayer.